A

Distortion

Of

Reality

By

J. A. Pickett

The opinions expressed by the author are not necessarily those of Revival Waves of Glory Books & Publishing.

Published by Revival Waves of Glory Books & Publishing

PO Box 596 | Litchfield, Illinois 62056 USA

www.revivalwavesofgloryministries.com

Revival Waves of Glory Books & Publishing is committed to excellence in the publishing industry.

Published in the United States of America

Paperback: 978-1-387-03487-1

Table of Contents

Introduction

A Distortion of Reality is a reality of a different kind.

But whose reality?

Yours?

Mine?

Ours?

Forward

There are no character names or gender definitions in this book. I leave it strictly up to the reader's imagination. I know each time someone reads this book; each character will be different.

Chapter 1

The reason why I act the way I do is really very simple. But first, you must be a good listener. Secondly, what I tell you, you must accept as the facts, exactly as you are told. The third and most important, you must be caring. I will try to explain so you will understand; the best possible way will be from the beginning.

Listen and don't say anything until I'm done. Do you understand? You do? Good! I hope you don't mind, it is going to be a long explanation. Oh, so you already have a question? Well, go ahead and ask. Stop your stuttering and just ask your stupid question, will you! No wait! My frustration shows, dominating me at times. I do apologize for that sudden outburst. It would be best for you to just listen and this is my story. Close your eyes and join me as I take you on a journey you will never forget. Live it with me as if you were there.

Suddenly, it is happening, totally overbearing the evening. Now it is gone. Like a flicker of light from a candle being blown out. They are taking me away. I haven't done anything wrong! Or so I thought. There is no one to help us escape. Questions started to arise in my head; but I have no answers. There was no reason for all this. No reason at all, but they came, and they keep coming by the thousands. No one can stop them. The takeover is happening all at once. I keep wondering if it all has been preplanned. No one could stop these "soldiers". Soldiers from hell - that is a better description. I guess that is what they are. I do not know. All I know is that I can't scream, no matter how hard I try. I just can't. Is this some kind of horrible nightmare?

They thrash around and around us like we are some kind of savage beasts. Those animals! Oh! How I wish that I could do something to stop them and this madness! Darkness is all around. No more flickers of light can be seen, just masked faces, unafraid of anything. I ask myself, "Are they really humanoid or are they something else?" I wish I could see their faces to know my answer and then spit into their faces to show my hatred. Oh! How I hate them! I know not where I am, but I know it is as bleak as a sewage gutter. It's a dingy, cramped hole I assume. I think I'm going to be sick because of the disgusting odors that surround me. I can hear screams from the others even though I have not seen any of them since the soldiers first came and took us.

I feel a needle or something with the same feeling going into my arm. I fade into nothingness. I awake in a beautifully well-lit room where I am strapped to a table. There in my arm a needle was stuck into my vein and the constant sound of the drip, drip, dripping could be heard. I didn't know what was going into my system. It's a mossy green, stagnant looking liquid from what I can see.

Then suddenly, the sound of the dripping stopped. All I can feel is the sensation that backbone is about to be broken. Am I dreaming or is this really happening? I wish they would stop. I open my eyes and the pain has stopped. I don't know if it is day or night, or how long I have been here. It must have been months; months of sheer torture. I don't know if I had confessed to anything or not. I haven't done anything to deserve any of this! I am the living dead! I jerked suddenly and felt the extreme pain again. I lay still, controlling my movement. The pain has stopped.

I guess it's been a few hours later and I'm in another dark room. I don't know how I got here. But here I am, alone at last. I can hear the constant stomping of iron clad boots outside the door of my cell. I am very sore and oh so tired. But I know I cannot sleep; for if I do, I do not know what would happen to me.

They come into the room and drag me away. I do not know where we are going, but it is down a darkened hallway. We come to the end of the corridor and go into this dimly lit room. They toss me onto a cold metal table as if I were nothing more than a grotesque dog. The pounding of my heart echoes within me. I am afraid that the sound could be heard. I start to hear silent voices all around me and I wonder if they can hear them too. But how could this be? I start saying to myself over and over, 'I am one". Maybe that's what they want me to think. I start feeling strange all over during this torture session. I don't know why I feel this way, but it is as though someone or something is entering my body.

I guess it was several hours later that I find myself in another well-lit room and the brightness hurts my eyes. I am unaware of my fate. I lay there very still. I feel the perspiration running down my back. I feel as though I have been working out at a gym or something. I hadn't noticed that the temperature was extremely cool until I felt a sudden within me. I can't complain about anything; for if I do, I might be beaten or worse. Oh! The agony of it all! Especially not knowing where I am or what has become of me.

Then suddenly someone called to me, "Hey 452, get over here now! We are going to room 333." I know my fate at last. I have heard rumors about this room. They call it the 'Room of Darkness'. That once you went in there, you don't come back as you. You may look like you but that's about it. First, they give you a number and then you become like them. I am becoming a non-person or a hubot (human robot). I'm losing my total self. I can't lose my identity. I just can't let them do this to me. Oh, won't anyone help me. I need to escape this horrible place of bizarre and barbarian treatment but I know that's impossible because it is heavily guarded. One false move and your fate is decided instantly for you. It will be a slow and painful process. I hope I live through this unfathomable hell. Even if I do live through this, I know that my life will never be the same again. What am I going to do? I am losing my identity and becoming just another number in this very strange new world.

They fling me into a dark, restrictive, rancid hole. I am safe for now from those horrid, repulsive creatures. At least, I'm free to think for a while. Oh, what am I to do? At least, they didn't completely erase my identity. Maybe I can save what is left of my identity. I found a morsel of food on the floor and ate it. It tasted disgusting but I didn't care. I am starving. I need more food but there isn't any. My thoughts are suddenly shattered. They came and dragged me down a long, dark corridor and threw me onto a cold, metal table while a sudden chill runs down my spine. They strap my arms and legs down on the table and my head is placed in a vice-like device. All I can do is stare at the ceiling. There, spinning above my head with varying speed is a large, metallic, bright, shiny pointed object. It just keeps spinning and spinning, faster then slower, then faster as I become mesmerized by it. I feel as though I am entering another dimension - another world. It fascinates me with idle curiosity as I watch it. I seem to feel as though I'm floating through the air. My spirit is set free, but only for a moment. Then all hope ends as I hear the stomping of boots coming closer and I come back to reality. They come closer and closer. Maybe this is my chance to escape. I thought how can I when this place is so heavily guarded and I'm still strapped down on this table. I thought and thought until my head ached and my eyes felt as though they were going to pop out of my head to relieve the pressure that was building inside me. One strap came undone. Could this be magic? I wondered about that. Maybe I have extraordinary strength. How can that be since I haven't eaten in such a long time? How did it happen and why? I wish I had some answers from questions that keep arising. Then, suddenly, I heard voices saying.

Paranoia will destroy ya,

We will be coming for ya,

Soon...

They kept saying it over and over, again and again until I am saying it with them as though in a trance, becoming one with them.

Chapter 2

The bell rings; it is morning, finally time to awaken from this horrible reoccurring nightmare. At least, I feel as though I have been through this before? I am so totally confused, feeling weird and emotionally off balance. I will never tell anyone about these dreams. They might think I'm insane. I might be. But that's silly, right? I'm a top executive for the biggest corporation in the world, probably even the universe. Yes, I do believe that other worlds exist.

It's nine o'clock in the morning and I just finished eating breakfast. I think I'll walk to work today since it is so nice and warm. On my way, I passed a building I've never seen before. It appears I have seen it somewhere before. Now I remember - it was in my dreams. Strange, I guess. Maybe some kind of déjà vu.

This reminds me of the little red spot on my arm that I noticed this morning as I was dressing. My arm was a little sore and I was rubbing it. It was just a nightmare. Right?

Sitting at my desk and staring for a moment at the pile of papers, I take the top sheet and read it. It just needs a few adjustments on figures and statements made by a public official. I almost forgot to mention the department I work for is the Department of Literature or Litter-Dept. as it is always referred to. We take statements that were possibly said maybe a week ago and make it as if it was said today. I took the top sheet and read it. It just needed a few minor adjustments on the facts and figures that were stated by a public official. This is what I do five days a week. Sometimes, I must work weekends when there is an important gathering coming up during the weeks ahead. But that's a rarity.

The bell rings at noon; time for lunch. We usually have some kind of brown looking substance (I think they called it meat) and a murky liquid (coffee) to drink. *As you have probably guessed by now, I am not from your time and place therefore from this point forward I will refer to foods and other material items in terminology used by you to make it easier for you to understand what I am talking about.* I go through the line and find an empty table to sit at.

A few minutes later, I'm joined by a friend of mine. Unfortunately, (for a reason I can't explain) I cannot remember a name. We started talking about an article in the Party's newspaper. I thought about telling my friend about the dream that I had last night. But I decided it is best that I don't say anything. I wish I had someone I could talk to about that terrifying nightmare. It is still nagging me. I find its becoming harder and harder to keep the torturing subconscious within me and keep the look of the party on my face.

The bell rings again, time to go back to work. I walked back on the same street as I had done a hundred times before but it felt different. I don't know why, but it does. I returned to my desk where there was another pile of papers. It seems like an endless cycle that will go on forever.

It's fifteen thirty and quitting time finally. I can hardly wait to get home because tonight My Love will be there at nineteen hundred. I decided to skip dinner and get ready for the moment when My Love arrives and we become one. The time is finally here at last. I went downstairs and had my card punched by the one on duty. This allows them to turn their listening and seeing devices off because what is done behind closed doors, on your day is by law, their duty to allow you to indulge in any pleasure or desire you choose.

My Love is finally here. We are one at last and everything is alright once again. We embrace and kiss one another. I even forgot about that dream. It seems silly at this moment. We fall onto the bed after a long while and just laid there with the sheets covering us and just held each other. I glanced over at the clock and noticed it was time for My Love to go. I wish My Love could stay here forever. We held and kissed each other for a long moment. My Love told me goodnight and that we'd meet at the cafeteria in the morning.

"Is there something wrong?" My Love asked before leaving.

"No. Why do you ask?"

"You don't seem to be yourself tonight. You seem a bit distant."

"I'm just probably tired from the workload I had today; nothing to worry about."

My Love leaves and I'm alone again. I started getting ready for bed. I hope those nightmares don't plague me again tonight. I fell asleep with the feeling of serenity, knowing all is well.

It's about three a.m. and I awake suddenly in a cold sweat. An eerie feeling surrounded me. I don't know why. I tried to get up for some water but I couldn't. It felt like something was preventing me from getting to that pitcher of water. I decided to just lie back down and get some sleep.

I looked at the clock on the wall and its six-thirty in the morning. I didn't sleep much. I was getting ready for work when the phone rings. I picked up the receiver but there was no one there. Maybe I just thought that the phone rang. I knew right then and there it was going to be one of those days.

My Love was waiting for me downstairs when I arrived and asked me, "What's wrong? You look like hell."

"I know but I didn't get much sleep last night," I replied and that I'll talk later at lunch.

I skipped breakfast and went into work early. I really didn't want to be there. I didn't know where I wanted to be, just somewhere, anywhere but there. I also knew the penalty for skipping work for no good reason. It varied for each infraction that an individual committed. It might be a slap on the wrist by one of the whip masters or it could be much worse than anyone could ever imagine. So, I went on to work but my heart wasn't in it.

I arrived five minutes early and there was a pile of papers on my desk. I had just sat down when over the loud speaker the voice of our leader announced that there was a mandatory meeting of all party members at seventeen-thirty in Auditorium 7. That means I had no choice, I had to go even though I didn't want to. Of course, our leader will be there; over the loud speaker only. No one has ever seen our leader and probably no one ever will. The announcement was finally over and it was time to start working again.

It's five minutes until lunch and I finally finished the pile of papers. I got a chance to relax for just a bit and went to get a glass of water. When I got back, there was another pile of papers. I wonder sometimes if it will ever end but I know it won't. The bell rings and it's time for lunch.

I'm not really hungry but I go and get something to eat anyway. I saw My Love but My Love didn't see me. That was fine with me. I just wanted to be alone anyway. I finished my lunch and went back to work.

On my way back, I noticed that there was some commotion going on. I really didn't pay any attention to it. Finally, I arrived back at work and started sorting through the pile of papers and put them in some sort of order. My mind wondered just for a second to the scene I saw only moments ago. It bothered me a bit. Just for a moment. I had more important things to do than worry about it. Someone came by and laid another stack of papers on my desk. I hadn't even started looking over the organized piles; I can see there will be no let up today.

It is fifteen-hundred hours; time to go home and get ready for the meeting. We always get off a couple of hours early whenever our leader calls one of these meetings. They want you to take care of any business you might have. I went home and sat in my big comfortable chair for a few minutes. I looked at my watch and noticed that it was time to go to the meeting.

I arrived at the auditorium and sat in the back row. My Love sat next to me and didn't say a word. My Love just held my hand and the world outside of us didn't seem to matter. The topic was about the changes that the Party was going to making in the next few weeks. They stated that some of the members were not conforming to the standards set forth in the Doctrine which was adopted many years ago. Stronger enforcement policies were expected to resolve that problem. The meeting finally ended at twenty-hundred. My Love walked me half way home and we just stood underneath a street lamp. We gazed into each other's eyes for a long time. We said goodnight and went our separate ways. I had a wonderful feeling inside. I can't describe it but it is there. I go to bed knowing all is well.

Chapter 3

It's been a couple of weeks since my last entry. Nothing has been really happening. My Love calls me a lot but I never return any of the calls, we have seen each other quite often during this time. The nightmare hasn't returned. I went to work this morning as I always do. But this time it seemed different.

There on my desk is a small package with a note attached. At first, I thought it was from My Love but it wasn't. I read the note which had no signature. All it said was, 'I hope you have a bright and cheery day'. I asked a few people if they saw anyone leave this package on my desk. But they said they hadn't seen anyone all morning. I finally open the package. I cannot describe what was inside the package but it was gorgeous. I have never seen anything like this before, not even in any of the books I have read. I know I walked around all day with a huge smile on my face.

It's lunch time and I ate my usual. I know I must avoid My Love today. I just don't feel like being bombarded with questions or even talking for that matter. I've seen The Other One from a distance but luckily, I wasn't seen. It is time to go back to work. A note is laying in the middle of my desk. I read the note which was signed by The Other One. I thought for a moment of who that was and remembered it was the new hire from down the hall. I must admit that I noticed

The Other One from the first day becoming very intrigued and wanting to know a lot more about The Other One but I knew that I mustn't dare act on these thoughts. Still though, I can't help wondering about The Other One.

The time is four o'clock; quitting time. As I started to leave, I felt a tap on my shoulder, it was The Other One. We talked for a while and I told The Other One that I really enjoyed our talk. We said good-bye and went our separate ways. I went to dinner but I didn't see My Love. I was glad in a way; I really didn't feel like talking.

I'm finally home and very tired. I was getting ready for bed when the phone rang, it was My Love. I told My Love that I was too tired to talk and that I would call back later. I hung up and went to bed. I dreamed of The Other One. I wish these dreams would come true instead of the nightmares that I have been having. Perhaps, someday soon they will.

It's morning already and couldn't wait to get to work. I want to see The Other One even if it's from a distance. I got to work as quickly as I could. I decided to skip breakfast and hurried to work. There, down the hall was The Other One. The Other One looked my way and smiled. This is going to be another wonderful day. I get to my desk and there was a note from my Svisor (what you would call a supervisor). I went to the office and knocked on the door and was told to come in and have a seat. We discussed the documents that were to be changed before the election next month. The Svisor wants me to oversee the whole operation of changing the documents with new information. I went back to my desk to work on a pile of papers. I must finish this pile today so I can start getting these documents ready for printing. I knew for the next several weeks that I may have to work late and on the weekends until I finish with the project that has been entrusted to me.

Its noon and I go to lunch. No sign of My Love. I'm glad in a way that I didn't see The Other One either. I really didn't feel like explaining the happiness I felt and this foolish grin to either of them. It would be quite uncomfortable. I ate my lunch and went back to work. Another note was on my desk and it was from The Other One, wanting to talk to me after work. I finished working on that pile of papers. Ten minutes remained until quitting time. It seems like it is taking forever for the bell to ring. I straightened up my desk and it's finally time to leave.

I meet The Other One at the bottom of the stairs. The Other One wants to meet me at the Park of the Ancient World at thirteen-hundred tomorrow. I said I would be there and then bid a goodnight and went to dinner. I hurried home and went to bed early. I just couldn't wait until tomorrow. It was hard to fall asleep much less stay asleep because I was so excited to finally be alone with The Other One.

I woke up just before the bell rang, got out of bed and quickly dressed. I went and had some breakfast then back to my apartment after I finished eating. Since it was Saturday, I had some time to myself. I sat down in one of my chairs and started reading a book. The phone rings just as I was getting interested in that book. It was My Love.

My love said, "I really want to see you today."

I told My Love that I couldn't because I had made other plans and they couldn't be broken. I couldn't tell My Love the truth. Not yet anyway. It would devastate My Love. I told My Love that we would talk later and hung up.

It's twelve-thirty in the afternoon and I had started to go downstairs. I can't help thinking about The Other One. This is going to be a wonderful day! The weather is sunny and warm with a gentle breeze blowing. I finally get to the park; The Other One was there waiting for me and held me so close, so tight making me feel incredibly secure and comfortable. The emotions are intense and so right. I know what I must do and soon. We go through the gate holding hands. This is so wonderful. We found a secluded spot and sat down embracing one another.

I feel a gentle squeeze on my thigh. Oh! This is going to be a very memorable day. The Other One pulls me closer. And we start becoming one. We gently lay on our sides still holding one another. We slowly slip out of our coveralls. The Other One is so gentle, just the opposite of My Love. We dissolve into each other and fall asleep still in one another. I have never felt like this before.

It's a couple of hours later and I awake to The Other One's gentle kisses on my neck, warm lips sending heat into every part of me. It feels wonderful to be awakened this way. Our lips meet again; the kisses deep and very passionate. The Other One moves off slowly, pulling me up until we are both sitting; still locked in each other's arms.

It's night now and we decided to stay here in the park. This is great! The moon was full and bright, the clear night sky sprinkled with stars. I made a wish on the brightest star and knew that it was already starting to come true. I can feel that there is a huge smile on my face and contentment in my heart. I snuggle closer with my head on The Other One's chest, close my eyes and fall into a deep peaceful sleep.

It's Sunday morning and I hear the birds chirping and the warmth from the sun on my face. I feel The Other One move a little, nudging me slightly and embracing me gently. I really enjoyed waking up in the morning like this. We finally got up and dressed. But we take our time not wanting this moment to end, kissing passionately as we put each article of clothing on. We started walking arm in arm, stopping every so often just enjoying being together in such a quiet peaceful place. There was such a sweet smell in the air, you can almost taste it.

It's afternoon and we finally reached the entrance. The Other One decided to walk me home; still holding hands. I really didn't want this day to end. We arrive at my building and stopped at the bottom of the stairs. The Other One and I embraced, then kissed each other passionately and deep one last time. The Other One leaves telling me that I'll get a call when The Other One reaches home. I went upstairs and stopped at the main desk. The person on duty handed me a stack of messages. They were all from My Love. I went into my apartment and the phone rang. It was The Other One. We talked for a while then said goodnight and that we'd see each other in the morning. I hung up the phone and as soon as I did, it rang again.

My love was on the line and just yelled, "WHERE THE HELL HAVE YOU BEEN FOR THE PAST TWO DAYS!"

"IT IS NONE OF YOUR DAMN BUSINESS!" I replied and slammed the receiver down. I went to bed and fell asleep immediately. I dreamt of The Other One. I was happy and content. Even My Love couldn't destroy this feeling. I know My Love will try though.

Chapter 4

It's six thirty on this cool Monday morning. I got dressed for work and walked downstairs. It was chilly outside but I didn't mind one bit. All I could do was think about The Other One. I looked in the distance and saw My Love coming this way. I hurried to the cafeteria and lost myself in the crowd. I felt a tap on my shoulder and when I turned around it was My Love. I just stared at My Love not being able to believe the nerve to approach me after what was said on the phone last night.

"I'm so sorry for what I said last night," My Love said.

"I accept your apology. We really need to talk," I said.

"Can you meet me at the library at eighteen hundred?" My Love replied.

"Yes," I answered.

We departed. I finished breakfast and then hurried to work. There, waiting at the entrance was The Other One. We quickly embraced and went upstairs. The Other One and I departed in the hallway. I went to my desk and started working on the documents for next month's election. I started proofing the first stack of papers to see if any changes needed to be made. The first twenty pages had only minor changes such as dates and statistics. I started to read the twentieth page. All the quotes had to be changed since that person disappeared. It was as in if they never were in the first place. No one knows or is ever told what happens to someone that no longer exists. There are speculations on what happens to a person but no one has ever been able to prove it. I finally finished that first stack of papers and looked at my watch. I had five minutes until lunch. I straightened up my desk and went to lunch.

I went to the cafeteria. I saw The Other One who asked me to sit at that table but I said I couldn't today. The Other One was very understanding, unlike My Love who would have thrown a fit if I refused to sit at the same table. I ate my lunch quickly and hurried back to the office. I know that I must see My Love tonight. This was it, the moment I have been dreading the most. But it must be done tonight. I started working on the next pile of papers. At least by keeping busy, I won't have to think about it. I finally finished the stack of papers and turned for just a second when someone walked by and dropped another pile on my desk. Hmmmm. I began to wonder when this year's election was going to be. The party officials never tell us when it will be held until two days before. I looked at the clock on the wall and saw that it was quitting time.

I skipped dinner and went straight to the library. My Love was there waiting for me. We found a quiet corner and sat down. I told My Love that I'd been seeing someone else. That I was so sick and tired of feeling like a piece of property, having to tell about everything I was doing including explaining my whereabouts.

My love replied, "I must confess that I too have been seeing someone else."

I was surprised at first then a little angry but that quickly passed. Little did we know that we were being monitored. We continued the discussion and we both agreed that it would be best that we never see each other ever again. Since we weren't married, it isn't against the law to split-up (as the ancients would call it). I am relieved that this is finally all over with so I can now concentrate on The Other One. We hugged one last time and went our separate ways, neither of us looking back towards the other.

I hurried home hoping I wasn't being followed. I reached my building and stopped. I thought I heard footsteps. Looking around I saw nothing out of the ordinary. It was just my imagination. Or was it? I don't know anymore. Reality and what I think is real swirl together. I go upstairs and straight to bed. Maybe this was a bad dream and when I wake up in the morning everything will be alright.

It's about two in the morning when I wake up screaming and soaked in a cold sweat. The sound of my terrified voice is what woke me. Those horrid nightmares have returned. I thought that was all over with. This time they were more terrifying than when they first started to appear. It's as if someone is purposely doing this to me. But how can that be? I pondered this for a while until I fell back asleep.

It's time to get up. I decided to go and see the doctor instead of going to work. I got there and sat in the waiting room. There was only one other person ahead of me. I explained to the doctor that I was having a little trouble sleeping at night and that sometimes I would awake in the middle of the night in a cold sweat. I didn't dare go into the details of my nightmares for fear of what would happen to me. The doctor gave me a note to take a few days off from work and some medicine to take before I go to sleep each night. The doctor also suggested that I get involved in more Party activities as the doctor was glancing at my chart. I took the note and medicine and stuffed them in my pocket.

I glanced at my watch and noticed that it was almost time for lunch. So, I headed towards the cafeteria. I got in line and went inside. I finished my lunch and went straight back to my apartment.

A package was in front of my door. I hurried inside and opened the box. It was from The Other One. I read the note inside which said, 'I hope you feel better soon. I miss you.' I wondered how The Other One knew I wasn't feeling well. I sat in my chair and starred out the window. I started daydreaming about The Other One. I glanced at my watch and noticed it was time for dinner.

I wasn't hungry but I knew I had to eat something. I went to the cafeteria and got something small to eat and a glass of water. I went back to my apartment and got ready for bed. I took one of those pills that the doctor gave me. I slowly drift into a deep, restful sleep. I had a wonderful dream about The Other One.

It's morning and I awoke very well rested. The nightmares seemed to have disappeared, hopefully for good. I got dressed and hurried to the cafeteria. I was quite hungry since I didn't eat much last night. I found a table and sat down. I finished my breakfast and hurried to work. I gave the doctor's note to my Svisor who was glad that I was back. I passed The Other One in the hall on my way to my office. As I passed The Other One, I whispered that I wanted to talk at lunch. The Other One smiled and nodded as we went to our offices. There was a huge stack of papers on my desk waiting for me since I was out for a couple of days. I got all the papers sorted into order. I read the first page; all that was needed were some spelling errors corrected. I was half way through the stack when someone walked by and dropped off more paperwork.

I glanced at the clock on the wall and it was five minutes to twelve. I straightened up the stacks of paper on my desk until the bell rang. I went down the hall where The Other One was waiting for me. We walked to the cafeteria and got our lunches. We found a very secluded table where no one could see or hear us and sat down.

"Would you like to come over to my apartment tonight and spend the weekend?" I asked. I can't believe I had the nerve to ask such a thing. I would have never have asked my Ex to come over. Somehow this just seems to feel oh so right.

"Sure. I'll be there at seventeen thirty."

We finished our lunch and headed back to work. The Other One said in a whisper, "I'll see you tonight. I can hardly wait to hold you again."

We gazed into each other's eyes for a moment then went into our offices.

I sat down at my desk and started working on that stack of papers again. I'm so glad it is Friday and I get the weekend off. I glanced at the clock; almost quitting time. I finished the last page and straightened up my desk just before the bell rings. I saw The Other One was already out the door. I went to the cafeteria and ate something quickly then hurried home.

Before I went upstairs, I stopped at the desk and gave my card to the person on duty, informing them that I'll be having a guest staying with me the whole weekend. We can have someone stay with us one weekend a month. I hurried upstairs and got ready. I looked out the window for a moment before I closed the curtains.

It's seventeen-thirty finally and I heard a knock on the door. I said come in. As soon as The Other One came in and closed the door, I rushed into those waiting open arms and was embraced like never before, holding so tightly, kissing ever so passionately.

We walked over to the couch still holding hands and sat down. The Other One took out this odd-looking ring and placed it on my finger. We hadn't been together that long for something like this to occur. It usually only happens months or years later. I was in shock but only for a moment when I noticed that The Other One was already wearing that same ring. I knew what this meant as soon as we locked hands and the rings locked as soon as they touched. We have become one on all levels. This only happens when heart and soul of the two parties are truly meant to be one. No ceremony or any rituals are needed, unlike the ancient ones had to endure. Once you become one with someone, it is for life. There is no such thing as 'divorce'.

My New Love says with a self-satisfying grin, "I made a stop at the desk before I came up here and took care of some things."

"What did you to do?" I asked.

My New Love answers smiling, "I gave them a document that allows me to live here with you. The person at the desk also gave me a key to the apartment."

I was a bit shocked and wondered why My New Love would have done such a thing without talking to me first. Then with excitement, I beamed with joy and we started kissing so deep and passionately, with the feelings we have in becoming one in the same flooding my entire being.

Suddenly the phone rings causing a small interruption. My New Love answers and asks, "Hello, may I help you?" Then proceeds to tell the one on the other end you may not speak to My Luv and to never call here again and then hangs up the phone.

"Who was that on the phone?" I asked.

Then My New Love says, "It was someone who claimed that you two were still together and had a right to talk to you."

"Oh. That was my Ex, still delusional." I said.

"I took care of it and you'll never be bothered again," My New Love said.

We went back to where we left off not letting that phone call ruin the evening. My New Love glanced at the clock on the wall and noticed it was getting late. We got up from the couch, holding hands with the rings locked and went to bed.

Chapter 5

I woke up a little before the alarm clock goes off. I glanced over and saw that My New Love is still asleep. It was a wondrous sight for my eyes to behold. I still can't believe all that has happened over the weekend. We are permanently one and will be forever.

The alarm finally goes off and My New Love awakens. We get out of bed and get ready for work. We hurried downstairs and go to the cafeteria to get a quick breakfast. As we were walking to work I noticed my Ex was coming towards us and thought to myself now what; it's been over for a long time.

I looked over at My New Love and whispered, "Let me handle this."

My New Love just smiled and nodded in agreement.

My Ex stopped in front of us and just stood there about to say something. I spoke first not leaving a chance for my Ex to say a word. I said, "I DON'T HAVE TIME FOR THIS! Besides it has been over for a very long time and you need to just go and leave me/us alone. My New Love and I are one forever and there is not a damn thing you can do about it. Do you understand?"

My Ex stood there speechless and nodded that what I had just said was understood.

We continued on our way to work when suddenly My New Love stopped, pulling me close and kissed me so passionately that my knees felt weak. I looked up and saw that smile.

My New Love whispered, "The way you handled your Ex really turned me on. I can't wait until this evening."

We finally got to work and went into our offices. I sat down at my desk and started working on one of the several piles of papers. I know I had a huge grin on my face and I will try my best to hide it.

I'm half way through the first stack of papers and noticed that it was almost time for lunch. The bell rings and I decided to get something out of one of the machines downstairs instead of going to the cafeteria. I have a lot of work to get finished before the end of the day and I really didn't want to see my Ex and have to deal with that whole thing again.

I finished eating and went back to my desk to finish the stack from this morning. The bell rings again ending lunch. I had already started on the second stack when someone walked by my desk picking up the finished stack of papers and left me another one to complete by the end of the day. I finally finished all the stacks of papers on my desk and had just enough time to tidy up a bit.

I was about to get up as the bell rang when I felt a tap on my shoulder. I turned around and as I looked up saw it was My New Love smiling at me. I saw that all too familiar gleam in those eyes that I adored so much. I got up and My New Love took my hand as we walked out of the building.

We went to the cafetorium instead of the cafeteria. Only certain chosen people can eat here. The food is much better and we don't have to pay for it. From what I have read in a book about how things once were, this was considered by the masses to be an elitist type of club that only allows certain people of certain stature inside. It is still elitist in a way but it is not kept secretive at all. No one who is not a member can say or do anything to club members or enter the building itself. If someone does anything, it means certain and instant death. It is handled as soon as the offense happens right then and there by the police.

We went inside and were taken immediately to a very private dining room and just before the door was opened My New Love said for me to close my eyes. Which of course I did and My New Love held my hand as the door was opened. As soon as the door closed, My New Love said to open my eyes slowly. I did and saw a beautifully set table filled with the most wondrous dishes. The room was lit only by candlelight and a fireplace looking object was on the opposite side of where we were standing. I turned around and looked up at My New Love smiling as I was being pulled close and kissed passionately.

My New Love says in this very soft seductive voice, "I told you what the handling of your ex did to me." All I could do was smile as we walked towards the table. My New Love pulls the chair out for me, then goes and sits down on the other side.

Chapter 6

It's Election Day finally. I attended the rally that morning. Then I went to the open voting forum. Someone in the audience voted against our great leader. The "police" appeared; abruptly grabbing and dragging onto the stage that disloyal one, where they proceeded to have an impromptu execution to the sound of the cheering crowd. The maddening frenzy grew even more as they announced the winner of the election. As expected, it was our leader for the fifth straight term. The crowd went wild with people tossing their fellow comrades in the air. It was a glorious sight.

Then suddenly, someone started shouting, "THEY'RE COMING! THEY'RE COMING TO GET US ALL!"

Everyone started running in all directions just to try and get away. I managed to escape for now. But some were not so lucky. They were dragged off like mangy dogs, kicking and screaming as they were taken away. I saw my Ex being dragged by the feet, trying to grab onto anything to prevent being taken away. I had a little smirk on my face and thought to myself that this is what my Ex deserved to happen, acting like such a fool in public and nearly causing a scene. I went back to my apartment and locked the door.

It's about three in the afternoon when I finally calmed down. My New Love came home and asked, "What's wrong?"

"I was at the open forum this morning and everything was going great. Then suddenly someone started shouting, *'They're coming to get us all,'* and all hell broke loose. People were running everywhere and some were even dragged away."

When I finally finished, My New Love pulls me close and says, "There is nothing for you to worry about. You are safe with me since we are one and they are only going after those who refused to conform to the Party."

It was getting late and I was so tired. We went to bed and I fell asleep with My New Love holding me close. I saw the sun rising through my window; it looked like a giant fireball in the sky and I'm glad morning is finally here. I got up, took a shower and got dressed. I didn't see My New Love anywhere as I'm going downstairs. I assume My New Love left earlier while I was asleep. I go on to breakfast alone. The streets seemed so barren. Then I remembered that today was volunteer day and that I'm supposed to be at some committee meeting after breakfast. I hurried to the cafeteria and ate very quickly. I don't want to be late and have to face the unspeakable. I arrived a little early and received my assignment. I must help change all the posters of our great leader. This is done after every election to show our support and to make sure the picture and wording underneath reflects the party's stand on any issue. Failure to complete this task will automatically get you beaten severely by fellow comrades in the courtyard which is in the worst part of town. I have only witnessed this happening when I was very young and didn't understand why this occurred. But I understand now and will make sure that this task is completed before lunch. We hung up the last poster when I heard the bell ring for lunch.

As I walked towards the cafetorium, I felt someone grab hold of my hand. I turned and saw that it was my Ex which caused me to stop dead in my tracks. I yelled, "ARE YOU OUT OF YOUR DAMN MIND? YOU WERE TOLD TO LEAVE ME THE HELL ALONE! WHAT DO YOU HAVE TO SAY FOR YOURSELF?"

My Ex stared at me with wide open eyes and started stammering to try to explain. I didn't want to hear the explanation, apology, or excuse; I just want my Ex to just get out of my face. I told my Ex in a very harsh and stern voice, "You do know what is going to happen to you when My New Love finds out what you did to me."

All my Ex could do was nod in acknowledgement and release my hand then hastily turned around and ran away like the coward I always knew my Ex was.

I quickly ate something and hurried back to work.

As I walked down the hall, My New Love was a little ahead of me but stopped and turned around. Upon seeing the look on my face asked, "What's wrong?"

I just stood there unable to answer hoping what just happened didn't really happen at all. My New Love realized by the look on my face that my Ex had something to do with me being upset and whispered, "Don't worry; I'll take care of everything. You won't be bothered by that animal ever again."

I looked up and smiled slightly knowing it'll be alright once again.

We went to our different departments just as the bell began to ring. I took the top page off the stack on my desk and started reading it making sure that there were no misspellings and the quotes were accurate. It didn't take me long to finish that stack when someone came by my desk and picked them up leaving me another one to work on. I started straightening up my desk before the lunch bell rang when someone came by and dropped off an envelope on my desk. I opened it and read, 'Meet me underneath the big tree across from the cafetorium for lunch.' I wondered who sent this and quite intrigued by this unexpected lunch date.

The bell rings and I head over to the big tree as quick as I could. I still had no idea who sent me that note. When I arrived, I saw My New Love sitting on a blanket with a basket full of food underneath the tree. I think this is what is called a 'picnic'. I had only read about people going on these things and seen a few pictures but I never thought I would be on one.

My New Love helped me down to the blanket and asked, "Surprised?"

"Yes. It's such a pleasant surprise," I answered.

We ate all the food in the basket and drank a few glasses of what looked like wine. We finished and got everything picked up and headed back to work.

Chapter 7

I got to the auditorium a little early. There were a few others already there. We took our seats to listen to a lecture about the upcoming changes. I started to cringe in the middle of the lecture but caught myself before anyone could see me. My heart sank as I knew that my horrid dreams were now a reality. I kept thinking about what My New Love said about how everything was going to be alright. The lecture was finally over and it's time for lunch. I had something to eat and went back to my apartment.

As I opened my door I saw what looked like flower petals all over my floor forming some sort of trail. So, I closed the door and followed the trail to my back bedroom. There was a note lying on my bookshelf. I read the note and all it said was, turn around slowly with your eyes closed.

As I was turning around, I felt a very light touch on my arm. I heard a soft whisper say, "Open your eyes slowly." I did and saw My New Love only dressed in a smile. It was the most fantastic night, in which there are no words to describe the emotions that I am feeling. The way My New Love took me and understood all those special places that my Ex didn't know about; making me scream like a banshee in heat. We fell asleep locked inside each other.

It's Monday morning and we got up before the bell rings. We decided to take a shower together. It was the first time that we had done this. I have read about people doing this in the ancient times and how the pleasure intensifies as the warm water flows over the body. I thought it was just fiction until this morning.

We hurriedly got dressed and went to breakfast at the cafetorium. When we got to work, we parted in the hallway and agreed to meet for lunch. I got to my desk just before the bell rang and saw several stacks of papers that needed to be organized. I knew that it was going to be a very long and tedious day. I started working on a pile that just needed to be checked and changing the stats, figures, or quotes making sure they are the most current and up-to-date. I must make doubly sure the quotes are accurate and have no spelling errors. One word misspelled or put in the wrong place could be disastrous not only for the person who spoke but me as well for making the mistake in the first place. I was half way through the second stack of papers when an announcement came over the loud speaker. Everyone stopped what they were doing and paid very close attention to what was being said. At the end of the announcement, we were told to be at the outside auditorium right after lunch. I knew this could mean one of two things and either way a bunch of arrested comrades were going to be publically executed. I finished the second stack as the lunch bell rang.

I met My New Love just outside the building where we work and went to lunch. We decided to go to the cafeteria instead of the cafetorium since it was closer to the auditorium. We finished eating and just sat there for a few minutes gazing into each other's eyes and not saying a thing. We do this often to keep us totally connected to each other's feelings and thoughts.

It's about one in the afternoon when we head towards the outside auditorium. We took our seats in the back just as the end of lunch bell rings. The first speaker came up to the podium and started talking about the big changes that were inevitably coming in the next few weeks. Also, that we must adapt and comply with what we are told and shown.

After the speaker finished, they brought in the first arrested comrade. They used the draw and quarter method as the chosen form of execution. The crowd went wild, cheering so loud that it drowned out the blood curdling screams. They brought in several more comrades and used various execution methods causing the crowd to go into a mad frenzy. They finally brought the last one in. It was my Ex. I turned away and couldn't watch. Unfortunately, I couldn't leave either. If I did, I would have been taken up there next. I could hear the screams coming from my Ex over the roaring crowd. I looked quickly and noticed that they didn't execute my Ex. It was much worse. There are no words to describe what they did to my Ex. I looked away again as they dragged all the bodies away.

My New Love looked my way and saw that I was trembling knowing that what just took place upset me greatly. We got up and left after it was all over. My New Love took my hand without saying a word. We went straight to the cafetorium where we had a suite waiting for us.

As the door closed behind us, I went straight to the bathroom where a hot bath was drawn and waiting for me. I undressed and lowered myself slowly into the tub. I leaned back and closed my eyes. The bath was so relaxing that I drifted into a light sleep and the events earlier that day seemed to just vanish as if they had never happened. I don't know how long I had been in the bath but I felt a gentle touch stroking my hair. I thought I was dreaming at first until I opened my eyes half way and saw My New Love sitting on the floor beside the tub. I smiled a little and closed my eyes again.

"How are you feeling?" My New Love asked in a soft voice.

I answered sleepily, "A lot better."

My New Love quietly got up and undressed then slowly eased behind me in the tub so not to disturb me. My head rested gently on My New Love's chest, neither one of us saying a word and My New Love's arms gently caressing my body.

Chapter 8

I came home from work but something just didn't seem right as I slowly opened the door. As soon as I closed the door behind me, I walked to the living room. Suddenly, out of nowhere, my Ex appeared. I stood there for a moment in shock.

As I re-gained my composer, I asked, "How the HELL did you get in here?"

My Ex replied, "There was no one at the desk, so I just came upstairs and opened the door with a key I had made some time ago so I could come in whenever I wanted to even when you weren't home."

"I NEVER GAVE YOU PERMISSON TO MAKE THAT KEY! NOW YOU HAVE REALLY DONE IT!"

Then suddenly the door opened and a gruff voice yelled, "STOP! DON'T MOVE!   We've got you now." The guards passed me, grabbed my Ex and threw the jerk on the ground. But unlike my dream, they weren't after me.

I felt a hand on my shoulder turning me around. It was My New Love pulling me close and holding me tight. My New Love whispered, "I got a call from the guard on duty that yelling was heard from our apartment. I hurried home as fast as I could. I can still feel you trembling, everything will be alright."

All I could do was wrap my arms around My New Love. I couldn't utter one word.

I heard my Ex yelling at the guards to back away. They didn't and told my Ex in a very gruff voice to stop that yelling or they will make it stop. The yelling continued and then I heard what sounded like a thwack, then silence. I turned my head slightly and saw the guards dragging my Ex by the legs of what seemed like a lifeless body. I had to turn my head away quickly after witnessing the horror.

I must have fainted because when I regained consciousness, I was lying on the couch. Sitting next to me on the floor was My New Love placing a cool towel on my forehead. I could tell by the look in those eyes how frightened and concerned My New Love was, about what just happened and my fainting, as well as the anger at what my Ex had done to me.

My New Love asked in a soft voice, "Are you ok? I was so worried about you."

I replied in weak and shaky voice, "I think so. I feel so drained and tired."

"Shhh. No more talking. You need to get your rest. I'll be right here next to you."

I drifted off to sleep again.

It is Monday morning when I wake up about an hour before the bell rings. I began to sit up when I noticed that My New Love wasn't there. I got up and headed towards what was referred to in a book I read as a kitchenette and saw what looked like breakfast on the small table. My New Love smiled as I sat down.

I exclaimed, "WOW!! What a nice surprise, so unexpected. You didn't have to go to all this trouble for me. Thank you so much."

My New Love replied, "You're welcome. It was no trouble at all; I really enjoyed making this for you. I figured after yesterday's events that you really needed a little pick me up."

I started eating the delicious meal and drank a juice like liquid. After I was done, I looked at the clock and noticed that we had to get dressed in a hurry to make it to work on time.

As we were walking to work, I glanced across the street. I thought I saw a couple of guards dragging what looked like my Ex by the feet. But then again, maybe I was just seeing things and hoping in a small way that it was my Ex especially after what happened yesterday. I will try to forget but I won't ever forgive that jerk for putting me through hell.

My New Love asks, "Is there anything wrong?"

"No. Everything's fine."

"Are you sure? You looked like you have something on your mind," My New Love said. We finally got to work and said that we'll meet for lunch.

I got to my desk and started sorting through the stacks of paper putting them in order. Someone came by my desk and told me that the Svisor wants to see me, now. I got up and went straight to the office.

Before I could knock on the door, I was told to come in. I sat in a chair that was in front of the desk not knowing why I had been called in.

"Congratulations on your promotion," the Svisor said.

"What promotion?" I asked.

"I received these documents this morning with your name on it stating that you have been promoted to a different department across the hall. You will report to that department after lunch."

I went back to my desk and started working on that stack of papers again trying to finish before lunch. I thought to myself that the department across the hall is where My New Love works. I finally finished the last piece of paper as the lunch bell begins ringing.

My New Love was waiting for me in the hall. We get outside when we stopped suddenly and My New Love asks, "Is there something wrong? You don't seem like yourself. You seem different than you were this morning."

I replied, "There's nothing wrong. But I just got some exciting news."

"What is it? Don't keep me in suspense," My New Love said. "I got a promotion and I start right after lunch."

My New Love looked surprised at first and said, "Congratulations. What department?"

"The department you work in."

Before anything else was said, My New Love grabbed me and pulled me close with arms wrapped around me, kissing me very passionately. Not caring if anyone saw us. Then releasing me, we headed to the cafeteria holding hands. We got our lunch and found a table and sat down.

After we finished, we got up and started to head back to work and My New Love whispered in my ear, "I know that animal won't dare come into this department. I will make sure of that."

I smiled as we continued walking.

Chapter 9

I go to my desk in my new department. It felt a little awkward at first but it quickly faded away. This department deals strictly with mostly books making sure that the stories fit today's society. The books are either fiction for entertainment or nonfiction written by political figures. Even classic novels are changed. I started reading my first book, highlighting the changes that needed to be made. I finished the first three chapters when the bell rings for the end of the work day.

My New Love came to my desk just as I stood up. We walked out together holding hands and went to the cafetorium. As we were walking, I thought I saw someone in the shadows but then they were gone. Maybe it was just my imagination playing tricks on me.

We got to the cafetorium and sat down in the dining area enjoying a very nice meal. My New Love raised the glass of wine and gave me a congratulation toast for the promotion I just got. After we finished eating, My New Love got up and sat down beside me and told me to close my eyes. When I opened them, I saw the most beautifully decorated cake that was carved to look like us. We finished eating our dessert and got up to leave, thanking the staff for such a delightful meal.

There was still a little daylight left as we started heading back to our apartment when suddenly my Ex jumped out of nowhere. My Ex angrily said, "YOU THOUGHT YOU COULD GET RID OF ME! YOU THOUGHT WRONG!" My Ex started coming towards me to do great harm.

Before I could utter a word, My New Love stepped in front of me and grabbed my Ex by the throat. My New Love yelled, "I TOLD YOU TO LEAVE US THE HELL ALONE! YOU LEAVE ME NO CHOICE BUT TO BEAT YOU TO DEATH!"

All I could do was stand there and watch in horror as My New Love started the brutal beating. There was blood going everywhere. I could hear my Ex screaming as the beating intensified.

It was starting to get dark and I could hear what sounded like guards coming towards us from a distance. They came quickly, pulling My New Love off my Ex. One of the guards saw that it was my Ex. The same one that had executed the public torture and exclaimed, "It's you! Apparently, you didn't learn your lesson from the punishment you received the other day."

The head guard came up and said, "Take this animal and tie it to the post over there."

The guards quickly did as they were told. One of the guards pulled out what looked like a rod, which was fully charged with electrical current, then placed it on my Ex's chest who then let out a blood curdling scream saying sorry to me and swearing to never bother us again.

The head guard comes to where my Ex is tied and said in a very gruff voice, "You should have thought about that before you did this tonight. You brought this all onto yourself." Then the guard pulled out what looked like a pistol that uses a high voltage charge and placed it against my Ex's head pulling the trigger.

I looked away as my Ex screamed one last time before falling to the ground taking one last breath. The guards took the body and tossed it into the dumpster like a piece of trash.

We decided to go back to the cafetorium instead of our apartment since it was getting late. We got to our suite and I went to the bedroom and lay down. My New Love got a hold of one of our Svisors to let them know what happened and was told we could take a few days off without penalty due to the circumstances of what had just happened. My New Love hung up the phone and came into the bedroom where I was and laid down next to me.

I finally fell asleep hoping that the events from earlier this evening never happened and it was all just a dream. Suddenly, I woke up screaming which startled My New Love out of deep sleep.

My New Love pulled me close and held me tight and in a whisper said, "Shhhh, it'll be alright."

I finally stopped screaming and said, "I just had the most horrific nightmare."

My New Love asks, "What's going on?"

"I was dreaming that I was watching guards pick up what looked like my Ex's lifeless body tossing it into a dumpster like it was a piece of trash."

"It was only a dream. Everything will be alright when you wake up in the morning," My New Love said. We fall back asleep with My New Love's arms wrapped around me making me feel safe and secure.

It's about a half past ten on a Sunday morning when I finally wake up and get out of bed. I could hear My New Love in the shower so I went to the living area. I saw this table with someone standing next to it. I was asked to come over there, get on the table laying facing down. I was curious and did as I was asked. I then felt strong hands started at my shoulders, working their way down slowly rubbing the muscles deep within me. I think this is called a massage. I have read about this procedure and thought it was just a story that had been written. I never thought the story was true until now. I can see why one would want to get a massage. It feels so good and relaxing. I closed my eyes, enjoying this immensely. I was asked in a soft voice to roll over onto my back which I did gladly, beginning at my neck and shoulders again those marvelous hands were working their way back down as before. I could get used to this and closed my eyes again.

When I opened my eyes again, My New Love was looking down at me with a smile and asked, "Did you enjoy your massage?"

"Yes, I did. Thank you so much," I answered.

"I knew that you needed something like this to help you relax and release all that stress that has occurred recently."

"You always know how to make me feel better. We are so in tuned to each other's needs and wants." I wanted to say, *"And where and how do you keep coming up with all these new ideas and things to please and surprise me?"* But I didn't.

My New Love helped me off the table and we got dressed. We went to the main dining room and had a light breakfast. Then we headed back to our suite for some much needed one on one time and let the front desk clerk know that we didn't want to be disturbed at all. This time it felt different. It is hard to explain. We were so tuned in to each other, much deeper than ever before. We fell asleep lying in each other's arms.

It's Monday morning when we wake up. We got up, dressed and then headed to the dining room for something to eat before heading back to our apartment. On the way, I noticed that there were a bunch of flowers blooming that were never there before. My New Love picked one and gave it to me. I smiled and took a quick sniff of the flower. I didn't know what kind it was but the fragrance was wonderfully sweet and very intoxicating. We continued walking, taking our time to enjoy the scenery. We finally get home and I put the flower in a glass of water. The whole room was filled with that wonderful scent. I went to the bedroom and started undressing to get ready to take a nice long hot shower; My New Love came up behind me not saying a word and did the most unexpected thing ever. Then went back to the living room and sat down on the sofa. I finished undressing and went to the bathroom to take my shower. As I walked by the mirror I noticed that there was something on my neck. I went to the living room where My New Love was sitting not saying a word. I saw the sly grin on My New Love's face and understood completely what the mark on my neck meant. I went back to the bathroom and took my shower. I finished and stepped out from the shower. I dried off and put on my robe then went to the living room.

When I looked over towards the kitchen I saw that the table was set with candles lit. There was this wonderful meal that was prepared by My New Love. My chair was pulled out by My New Love waiting for me. I sat down and said, "What a nice surprise."

My New Love said, "Happy First Anniversary Luvs." Then, without missing a beat pours each of us a glass of the finest red wine and serves me dinner first before taking a seat on the opposite side. We toasted and drank a little while eating this deliciously prepared meal. My thoughts wandered a little about My New Love calling me Luv. My New Love has never called me Luv or any special pet names before. It's a nice surprise. I quickly got all those insecure thoughts out of my head and just enjoyed the evening that we're having together.

After we finished eating, My New Love gets up and disappears to the back bedroom and says, "Close your eyes. I'm coming down the hall."

I complied and giggled a little with excitement. I can't imagine what was coming next. When I opened my eyes, My New Love was on one knee smiling the biggest smile that I have ever seen and holding this nicely wrapped present handing it to me. "Go ahead and open it. I hope you like it," My New Love says.

Chapter 10

It's Tuesday morning, time to get up and go back to work. It'll be good to get back and start where I left off last week. We get dressed and grab a quick breakfast on our way out the door. We get to our department just before the bell rings and said we'll see each other at lunch. I sat down at my desk and started reading the book I had started on just as the bell finishes ringing. I did a quick re-read of the previous chapter and notes that I had written to refresh my memory. Then I continued reading the rest of the book making all the necessary changes that were needed before sending it off to the RePrinProc Dept which stands for Reprint and Processing Department. This is where they will print all new books while destroying all copies of the old version. This is the way the party can keep total control over what is read and who is reading what.

I'm half way through the second book when someone walks by dropping an envelope on my desk. I put down the book and opened the letter. I started reading it becoming increasingly scared. It said:

I know where you live

I know who you're with

I know what department you're in

I know what happened last week

And who set up your Ex

I know who ordered the torture

I know you will be next

If I could have it my way . . . .

There was no signature or anything to identify who sent this letter. I hurriedly folded it up and stuffed it back into the envelope. Maybe this is someone's idea of some kind of joke and a very cruel joke at that.

The bell rings for lunch and I hurried out the door and didn't wait for My New Love like we had planned this morning. "Wait! Let me catch up to you." My New Love yelled.

I stopped and waited for My New Love to catch up to me. "Why didn't you wait for me? What's going on?"

I didn't answer. I just pulled out the letter I had received this morning and handed it to My New Love. I could tell by the facial expressions and body language that intense anger was to about erupt.

My New Love finished reading the letter and angrily said, "THAT BASTARD! Don't you worry about that letter I'll personally take care of everything."

We continued to the cafeteria and ate some lunch even though I wasn't really hungry. After we finished My New Love got up and made a phone call to someone, then came back and said, "I called our Svisor and explained what happened this morning and was told to tell you to take the rest of the day off and go straight home after lunch. Also, there is something for you to take on the kitchen counter to help you relax and rest."

"I wish all this would just end so that we could live a peaceful life. Somehow my Ex has managed to find a way to upset me even from the grave."

My New Love walked me home making sure that I made it without any problems and said, "I'll be home right after work." My New Love left and I went into our apartment. I took the medicine that was on the kitchen counter and went to bed. It didn't take long before I fell into a deep, blissful sleep.

I don't know how long I had been asleep but I awoke to My New Love's gentle kiss on my forehead. "How are you feeling?"

"I'm a lot better after getting some rest," I answered.

We decided to stay home for dinner. I tried to stand up to go to the kitchen to eat and felt a little weak. My New Love had come back to the bedroom to see what was taking me so long and saw that I was having a little trouble walking; instinctively wrapping one arm around my waist, steadying me so I could walk to the kitchen.

It took a little time getting there and I sat down in one of the chairs at the dining room table. I wasn't very hungry but I ate what I could. I guess it takes a while for the medicine to wear completely off. We finished eating and My New Love helped me to the sofa then went back to the kitchen to clear off the table and wash the dishes.

It's been a couple of days since the latest incident and I'm finally getting back to work. I was about to read the book I had started on when I get a call to go to the Svisors office. I go immediately and closed the door behind me. As soon as I entered the office, the Svisor told me to sit down and said, "Due to the recent occurrences I've decided that it will be in your best interest to have a private office. There will be someone at the desk in front of your office, since you are way too valuable a member of the party, the department and to me, to ensure your safety and will guarantee that absolutely no mail of any kind or people will be allowed to enter your office without being authorized by the secretary. Here are the keys to your office which is two doors down from this one."

I was stunned since I thought I was going to be terminated (and not in a good way). I thanked the Svisor and went to my new office.

There sitting at the desk was My New Love. I so surprised that I just went into my office and sat down behind this huge desk. My New Love came in and said, "The Svisor and I had long talk this morning about what has been going on. We both agreed to my suggestion that I would be the best one to be your sectary so that you won't get any unwanted mail or visits from people. I have also made arrangements to have everything moved into your new office."

I didn't know what to say. So, I got up and gave My New Love a big hug as I whispered, "Thank you." My New Love went back to the desk outside my office and I sat back down behind my desk picking up the book I had started on earlier this morning.

Chapter 11

It has been a few months since I have moved into my new office. I must admit that at first it felt a little awkward working so closely with My New Love. As time went on that feeling went away and it was like any other day at work. I happened to look up from the book I was reading and noticed that there was some commotion in front My New Love's desk. I couldn't really hear what was being said since the office door was closed. I thought about getting up to find out what was going on but decided not to and went back to the book I was reading making all the necessary corrections.

Suddenly, I heard the sound of boots hitting the floor in a hastily run. I looked up again with a slightly frightened look on my face. I saw a couple of police place a device over some guy's mouth to stop the screaming and two others grasping arms, forcing them behind the back then placed a handcuff like device on them causing even more pain due to the small spikes placed strategically on the inside all around the wrists making sure they were tight until you could see a little blood dripping down. The police dragged their prisoner away by the cuffs making sure they caused even more pain. I didn't see My New Love anywhere while all this was going on.

I went back to the book again trying to erase the image I had just witnessed from my mind and concentrate on finishing this book when the phone rang. It was the Svisor wanting me to report to that office immediately. I wondered what this could be about as I hurried down the hall.

As I entered, the Svisor asked me to close the door. When I turned around, I saw My New Love standing right beside the Svisor. I was at a loss for words and sat down in a chair that was in front of the desk.

The Svisor began to speak as I listened with such intensity and said to My New Love, "First of all I would like to congratulate you for the persistence in pursuing the person who was responsible for writing that letter by presenting you with the highest medal the party has to offer and for protecting our most valuable party member. Be assured that this person will be dealt with in the most severe punishment that the police can use to make sure others do not even think about trying something like this in the future."

My New Love said, "Thank you very much. It was an honor and duty to protect not only my Luv but also the party as a whole."

Then to the both of us the Svisor said, "You two will be allowed to take the next two and a half months off for your dedication and bravery. This is something rare that the party allows Svisors to do and this is a very unique occasion. Also, both of your jobs and private office are permanently secured for the rest of your lives. Now, you two go and enjoy yourselves. I will see you both when you get back."

After all was said and done we left as ordered to have a nice (what was once called) vacation. Before we left, I went back to my office to straighten up and lock the door. We headed out the door into the most invigorating spring like day.

It's late afternoon and we decided to eat at the cafetorium. We finally get there and were about to go to our suite when the person at the front desk stopped us with information that our suite was no longer available and gave us the keys to a new one. The desk clerk told us that the suite was located on the other side of the building and down a long hallway.

Saying our thanks we proceeded to walk to our suite. My New Love opened the door and we went inside, this one was so much bigger than the one we just had. I noticed that there was an envelope on the table at the far end of the room. I went over to the table and picked up the envelope and started reading it aloud.

'This suite has been chosen for the both of you in appreciation for the dedication to the Party and for your assistance in the apprehension of the person responsible in trying to destroy the Party's most valuable member. Your things from your apartment will be delivered shortly. This will be your permanent residence. Again, the Party thanks you both.'

Sincerely,

Svisor

We both stood there looking at each other in total disbelief. No Party member has ever received anything like this; not that either one of us know of anyway. There was a knock on the door and My New Love answered it.

Standing there were two operatives in coveralls with all of our belongings from the apartment. Without saying a word or even asking either one of us where we wanted everything; they just came in and started putting our belongings away. They seemed to just know where everything went right down to the smallest detail. They finished in no time at all and left just as quickly as they arrived without ever saying one word to either one of us. We found out later that they were the Svisors private movers, gardeners or any other jobs they are assigned. They never question any assignment and always do as they are told. They know that insubordination or deviation from a direct order is automatic death. The method would be chosen by the one giving the order.

It's almost dinner time so we change into something nice and go to this most elegant dining area. We no longer eat in the cafetorium (not that there was anything wrong with the food or atmosphere) but since we have achieved a higher status they feel it best that we eat here instead. We were taken to a very private area that was reserved just for us and were seated by a personal waiter who has been assigned to take care of our every need. We were each poured a glass of their finest red wines which is kept in stock and reserved for members in the highest status bracket allowed by the party.

The waiter left and we toasted to the most eventful and wondrous day we have had. Our meals were chosen well in advance made to the Svisor's specifications. Neither I nor My New Love knew what we were having for dinner and were pleasantly surprised when the staff started bringing out all that food.

Chapter 12

It took us a little while to settle into our new place. I had gone to the kitchen to get something to drink when I noticed that there was an unopened envelope on the counter. There was no name or return address anywhere on it. I finished drinking my glass of water as I picked up the envelope. I took it with me and waited to open it after I got to the living room where My New Love is sitting.

My New Love asks, "What do you have in your hand?"

"Some sort of letter." I gave it to My New Love who then opened and read it.

"Who is it from? What does it say?" I asked.

"It's from the Party's Ultimate Leader which states that since we are in the highest status allowed by the Party that it is our sworn duty to produce more party offspring," My New Love said.

"When do we start?" I asked.

"According to this letter, we start immediately."

We were both so extremely excited at this new order we could hardly contain ourselves. My New Love grabs me as clothes are literally flying all over the place and I was being pulled on top. We become one instantaneously as soon as we are inside each other. We can feel the throbbing intensify within each other with every movement. This felt so wonderful. There was one last movement as we both drifted off to sleep still inside one another. I wake ever so slightly and notice I am still on top; My New Love's arms are wrapped around me and as I move position ever so slightly it pushes us up inside each other further so that the both of us are much deeper than before. We both fall into a deep and sated sleep.

It's early on a Wednesday morning and I was awoken before My New Love. What a night. This was something I have always dreamt about, to have a night like I did last night. Unlike my dreams, last night was what someone would call 'mind blowing' and much more intense than anything I have ever felt before. I got dressed and went to the kitchen to make a pot of coffee. I heard the sounds of My New Love getting up. The coffee finally finishes and I pour each of us a cup.

My New Love comes in smiling like a Cheshire cat and asked, "How was it for you last night? It was fantastic for me."

"It was the same for me. I have never experienced anything like that before."

As we finished drinking our coffee, there was a knock on the door. I opened the door and a waiter wheeled in this table that had breakfast on it with all kinds of goodies to eat.

"I ordered this for us knowing that neither one of us wanted to go anywhere this morning," My New Love explained.

My chair was pulled out for me and I sat down. My New Love went to the other side and sat down. We finished eating our breakfast then got up and went to the living room. I sat down in a plush, curl up in it style chair that was nestled close to a window. I picked up a book style magazine, began scanning through it and found a very intriguing article. I glanced up a little and noticed that My New Love was lying down on the sofa and was reading the party's newspaper. I had such a feeling of absolute euphoria wash over me as if I am finally totally complete and whole.

A few months have gone by and time for us to go back to work in the morning. We have been very busy fulfilling our newly assigned duty and obligations (it has been such a pleasure for us) to the Party that we almost forgot we still have jobs.

Its six o'clock on a Monday morning and we get up just as the alarm clock goes off. We eat a quick breakfast then get ready for work. We go out the front door and there is a driver outside standing at attention next to a vehicle.

The driver says to us, "I'm here to take you to work", holds the door open and we get in without hesitation. If we didn't, there would have been some sort of consequence and that is something neither one of us wants to deal with. We finally arrive and I go directly into my office. My New Love had stopped by the Svisor's office for some reason. I opened one of the books on my desk and started reading it, highlighting what changes needed to be made. I'm about half way through the book when I hear a knock on the door. I say to come in and to my surprise, it was My New Love.

"I just wanted to let you know that I'm back from talking to the Svisor. I was expressing my thanks for everything we have been given," My New Love explained.

I went back to what I was doing and My New Love sat down at the desk in the outer office to work on some papers.

It's about lunch time when I was working on the last chapter that will need corrections. The bell rings and My New Love is waiting for me outside my office door. We walked outside the building and My New Love takes my hand without saying a word and leads me to a place I have never been to before.

It was in a very secluded area with very few people around. We are seated in a private booth that had been reserved for us. There were a couple candles lit on the table adding to the ambiance. The waiter brought the first of a seven course meal. The salad had fresh greens and vegetables that were lightly dressed in vinaigrette. The soup was brought out next. It was a cross between a tomato bisque and minestrone. The main course came out in three parts. The first was a rack of lamb, the second was prime rib and the duck was brought out last. These were all served with fire grilled potatoes, honey glazed carrots and endless glasses of the finest wines that have been paired with each entrée. Dessert was just as delicious. It was called 'Baked Alaska Surprise'. We finished everything and then I started not to feel right. Since we only had to work a half day we had our driver summoned to take us home.

Chapter 13

My New Love picked up the phone and asked the front desk clerk to be connected to the physician on duty since I wasn't feeling well. Within a few minutes the phone rings and My New Love answers. It was the doctor's assistant.

After My New Love hung up the phone, I asked, "Well. What did they say?"

"We need to report to the office immediately for testing."

We immediately rush over to the Dep-Hel (Department of Health) building where we were greeted by the staff. They ushered us in quickly and said, "We have been expecting the both of you."

The doctor examined My New Love first and found nothing wrong.

I was examined and the doctor says, "I will have to do further testing on you. I'm not sure what's wrong with you. I'll be right back."

My New Love followed the doctor out into the hallway where they started talking. I couldn't tell what was being said. The doctor hurriedly went down the hallway and My New Love comes back to the room I was in.

"What's going on?" I asked.

"Don't worry. There's nothing going on and everything will turn out fine."

The doctor comes back to the room I'm in and leads me down the hall. We go into this brightly lit room at the end of the hallway and I was instructed to lie down on the table. I did as I was told without any hesitation.

About thirty minutes later, a nurse came in with a bottle with liquid in it and proceeded to insert an I.V. into the vein of my left arm. It stung for a second then I felt the coolness of the liquid beginning to flow through my veins.

The doctor comes back in and instructs the nurse to inject some kind of blue-green liquid into the I.V. I slowly drift off to sleep not knowing what will happen to me next. I thought I heard whispers but maybe it was only my imagination. I started dreaming and saw myself on the outside looking in. I'm not sure what it all means. I could see my Ex in a room. I could see My New Love in some other room. Then I could see the two of them together being intimate with each other. I found that part of the dream a bit disturbing and at the same time fascinating. I saw myself with my Ex and then with My New Love, sometimes at the same time.

I didn't know how long I had been asleep or even what day it was as I began to wake up. It took me a little while to become fully awake. When I finally opened my eyes completely, the first person I saw was the doctor.

I was asked, "How are we feeling today?"

I answered in a groggy, tired voice, "Better. What day is it? How long have I been here?"

"Your questions will be answered later. Right now, you just need to rest," the doctor said leaving the room and I was alone again with my thoughts.

I wondered why My New Love hasn't come to see me. I began to drift off to sleep when I heard a knock on the door. This person was bringing me lunch. It's the first solid food I have eaten since I came to this place. The food didn't have a whole lot of taste but I didn't care I was just hungry. I finished everything on the plate and then someone came and got the empty tray.

The nurse came in a short time later and I said that I wanted to get up to walk around and was told that I will have to wait until the doctor gives approval before I can do anything.

The nurse left and the doctor came in soon after. I asked, "When will I be able to get up to do things like walking?"

"Perhaps tomorrow, we will have to wait and see how you are doing then. In the meantime, you will just have to rest and get your strength back, says the doctor and could see that I wasn't too happy about it but doesn't say anything more and just leaves. There was nothing I could do and I'm alone again.

It is a few hours later when I hear a knock on the door and I said, "Come in." When the door opened, it was My New Love.

"Why didn't you come and see me sooner?" I asked. "I was frightened and didn't know where you were."

"I was told by the doctor that it was best for me to wait until you woke up. You were sick and I was so worried about you. I didn't sleep much since you have been in here. I have missed you terribly and can't wait to get you home," My New Love said in a quivering voice.

I hadn't realized how sick I was until now. "I'm glad you came to see me and I have missed you too. The doctor says I might be able to get up tomorrow and begin walking so I can regain the strength in my legs."

My New Love hugged me gingerly and kissed my lips lightly and then said, "I'll be right back."

I smiled as My New Love left the room. I'm so glad that I finally had a visitor. I needed something to lift my spirits.

My New Love and the doctor return to my room a short time later. "I have some good news," the doctor said. "You're being moved to a private suite where you will be getting the best care and starting physical therapy tomorrow, this is effective immediately."

My New Love had a big smile and added, "The best part is that I will get to stay with you until you are released from here and I can take you home."

I was so surprised that I was speechless. All I could do was smile. The nurse came in with this wheel chair type device and put it close to my bed and helped me get off the bed and seated me in the wheel chair.

The doctor came over and removed the I.V. and said, "You won't need this anymore. You will have to take meds while you are here but they will be in pill form."

I was so glad that it has been removed and I didn't even mind that it left a small bruise on my arm from where it was inserted.

Chapter 14

We get on this elevator that took us to the top floor and then we went down this hallway. I noticed that there were about three or four suites on this floor. We finally get to the one we have been assigned. The nurse opened the door and wheeled me in first. Then helped me out of the chair and onto the bed making sure I was comfortable. The nurse gives the key to My New Love and leaves shutting the door.

The doctor comes in to see if I have settled in and if we needed anything. I noticed that there was another bed next to mine for My New Love to sleep on. The doctor leaves and there was a knock on the door. My New Love opened the door and there was an orderly wheeling in this small table with dinner on it and helped me get from the bed to one of the chairs at the table then tells us that I'll be checked on in a little while. My New Love sat down on the other chair that was at the table.

I happened to look down at my left hand and noticed that my ring was gone. Noticing this My New Love took my hand and placed the ring back on my finger. We interlocked our fingers making sure we are one once again and that we are completely in tuned with one another on every level.

"The doctor gave me your ring when you first entered here so it wouldn't get lost, understanding the significance and extremely high importance of this particular ring since very few people have this type of ring," my New Love explains. We unlock our fingers and began eating this wonderful meal. The orderly came back about an hour later to take the table and dishes away.

It was about nine p.m. when a nurse came in to help me into the bath tub and help me bathe. My New Love says that giving me a bath will be a pleasure. The nurse, with a look of understanding, leaves and My New Love helps me from the chair where I was sitting into the tub that was about half full of very hot but not scalding water making sure to lower me nice and slow so that I don't slip and fall. I'm glad My New Love was going to help me instead of the nurse, not that I would have had anything against it but I would rather have someone I know and feel comfortable with bathing me instead of a stranger. I finished bathing and My New Love helped me out of the tub and dried me off then helped me put my pajamas on before taking me back to my bed.

I was sitting on the edge of the bed when My New Love joins me holding me close while whispering sweet nothings in my ear. I lie down because I was starting to feel tired.

My New Love kisses me gently on the lips and says, "Goodnight, Luv. I'll see you in the morning."

Before the lights are turned off, a nurse comes in and gives me this small bluish pill with a glass of water then leaves after I take the medicine and My New Love crawls into the bed next to mine turning off the lights before falling asleep.

It's morning and I saw that My New Love had already gotten up. Breakfast must have been brought in while I was still asleep. My New Love comes over to my bed, helps me sit up and asks, "How are you feeling today?"

"I feel much better for the first time in a very long time."

My New Love then helps me get up and walk over to a chair at the table. I ate everything on my plate, I must have been a lot hungrier that I had realized. Someone came in a little while later to get the dirty dishes. I was still sitting in the chair and began reading an article in a magazine that was on the small table next to my chair. I found it quite interesting.

It was around ten thirty in the morning when we heard a knock on the door. My New Love got up and opened the door. There stood a therapist who looked to be somewhere in the late twenties or early thirties, not bad looking either, saying we were going to the DeptHab (Department of Rehab) for physical therapy. I was helped up from the chair where I was sitting and My New Love was told that we would be back in about two hours, in time for lunch. My New Love wanted to go with me but was told that wasn't possible.

We slowly walk out the door and down the hall to the elevator. All the while, I was being steadied by the therapist. We get into the elevator and go three floors down. When it fully stopped we got off and went into the rehab area. I was helped over to where these two bars are, instructed to get between them and hold on to them as I begin to slowly walk. I was a bit wobbly at first and almost fell. I finally got the hang of it and walked a little more steadily.

The therapist looked at the clock and said it was time to go back to my room and that I did very well for my first try. We walk to the elevator slowly as the attractive young therapist steadied me if I needed it and got in. We go back to the floor my room was on and walked slowly down the hall and then tells me that I'll be going back sometime in the afternoon for more therapy.

We reached my room and I opened the door, walking in slowly unassisted. My New Love was sitting in a chair as I walked in. I took another step towards the chair and almost fell. My New Love got up quickly taking hold of me before I fell and got hurt and said excitedly, "I'm so proud of you. I didn't think you would be able to walk without some assistance so soon."

Its twelve thirty and lunch was brought to us. I was hungry from this morning's physical therapy. I told My New Love that I will have to go back this afternoon.

"I'm not too happy about you having to go again so soon or the fact that I can't go with you," My New Love said in a distasteful voice.

"I know you're not happy about it but I guess the doctor feels that it is necessary that I do physical therapy twice a day so that I can get out of here sooner and back home," I explained.

"I guess I can understand the logic of why you have to go twice a day. I just can't wait until I can take you home," My New Love said.

We finished lunch and someone came and took the dishes. I sat in My New Love's lap and felt gentle kisses on my neck which I thoroughly enjoyed. I got up after a while and changed into some clean pajamas. My New Love started reading a book while I changed.

Chapter 15

It's about four in the afternoon when the young physical therapist from this morning knocked on the door. I opened the door and was asked, "Are you ready?"

"Yes, I am."

The Psvisor tells My New Love that we'll be back in three or four hours.

My New Love exclaimed, "Three or four hours! Why such a long physical therapy session?"

The Psvisor explained, "The doctor wants the physical therapy to be more intense so you can go home sooner."

As we went down the hall towards the elevator, leaving My New Love alone, I saw this tall red head knocking on the door to my room. My New Love opened the door and I could hear the nurse ask, "I was wondering when you were going to call for me."

My New Love said, "I just had to wait until the moment was right." Then the door closes quietly behind them. This upsets me tremendously.

I asked, "As we were walking, I glanced back and saw a nurse enter my room. Why is someone going in there?"

The Psvisor paused for a moment before answering, "The doctor finds that it's very beneficial that whoever is left in the room alone, while the one they are with is in therapy, isn't alone for a long period of time without some company. Sure, there are books to read but that can really mess one's mind up if all they do daily is read. So, a nurse is sent in to fill that time in with whatever the need is for them. The nurse stays until it is time for that person to come back from therapy."

After the Psvisor's explanation, I nodded even though in the back of my mind it just sounded more of an untruth. I also knew if the Party found out that I doubted what was told to me was absolute truth that I would be executed right on the spot.

I'm walking down the hall towards the rehab room. I turned to the Psvisor and asked, "Why are we the only ones in here?"

The Psvisor answered, "Everyone is assigned a personal physical therapist and reserve this room for a certain amount of time for them only, ensuring no distractions. In your case, I can reserve this room anytime no matter who has reserved it."

I went over and got onto this machine and started walking slowly, holding onto the bars in front of me. After about 10 minutes, the Psvisor sped it up a little bit making sure I was in a comfortable stride. I spent about another half hour on this machine. I was glad when the half hour was up and the machine had stopped because my legs were starting to hurt.

The young Psvisor asked me to follow. We went into the back office; I heard the door closing behind me then felt hot breath on the back of my neck sending goose bumps up and down my spine as I heard a whisper in my ear, this very soft and sexy voice, "I made sure that I got you as my patient. I have wanted you ever since the first time I saw you from a distance with Your New Love."

I was speechless at first and then I turned around slowly until our eyes met and locked. The Psvisor pulls me close, wrapping those powerful arms around me tight as I was being kissed from my neck working slowly towards my lips. I could feel the heated passion from those lips and felt the strong desire of want and need. The Psvisor spoke softly as I was lead to the couch that was on the other side of the room across from the desk. I followed without question or hesitation as my body was beginning to flame with a surprising yearning.

The Psvisor said, "I'll take this nice and slow. I want you to feel how intense my burning desire is for you."

We sit on the sofa and I said in a whisper, "I have never had anyone feel this way about me. We cannot let anyone know about this, especially My New Love."

The Psvisor removed the therapist shirt, exposing a tremendously hard muscled body, and then assisted me in removing the t-shirt I was wearing.

I asked in a whisper, "You never told me your name."

"It is just Psvisor."

I finished the physical therapy and was told I did an excellent job. We head to the elevator and went back up to my floor. As the elevator door opened and we got out I saw a red-headed nurse coming from my room. I wondered to myself why the nurse was still in my room. We walked down the hall and the Psvisor says, "I'll see you in the morning at ten a.m." Then turns and heads back to the elevator.

I opened the door to the room and My New Love is sitting in a chair reading.

"Why was the nurse in here?" I asked in a slightly annoyed voice.

"I just wanted someone to talk to while you were in physical therapy," My New Love answered.

I said ok but you could tell by the look on my face that I still wasn't too thrilled about it and went to take a shower. I got out, dried myself off and dressed. I decided not to say anything more about it. I finished in time for dinner.

Two months have gone by and I'm finally being released from the hospital and going home. A nurse comes to the room takes us to one of the exam rooms down the hall.

The doctor comes in and does a thorough exam then signs the release form then tells us before we leave, "Be sure to stop by the nurses' station to pick up the medications and to only take them if any symptoms begin to show again."

We expressed our thanks and went back to our room to begin packing. There was a knock on the door and when I opened it, the Psvisor and nurse were standing there. The Psvisor said, "The doctor wants you to have one more physical therapy session before you leave."

I went without hesitation because if I didn't the doctor could rescind my release making me have to stay longer. As we walked down the hall, I saw a nurse standing at the doorway and then entered the room. The nurse and My New Love embraced passionately with their lips together setting each other's soul on fire then close the door.

We got to the rehab room and I got on the walking device but I wasn't really trying. My heart just wasn't in it. The Psvisor stopped the machine and asked, "What's wrong? You don't seem like yourself today. You should be happy that you're getting to go home this afternoon."

"As we were walking, I glanced back and saw a nurse enter my room. I know you told me why someone goes there while I am in therapy. It is just upsetting for me."

Chapter 16

We finally got everything packed and headed to the front entrance where a car is waiting for us. It'll be good to finally be at home. My New Love is already inside the car and I was about to get in myself when I felt a hand on mine. I didn't turn around as I grasped onto what felt like a small envelope and heard a whisper in my ear, "Only open it when you are alone." I stuffed that envelope in my left pocket of the pants I was wearing and got into the car.

We are finally home and as soon as My New Love opens the front door, I started to head to the back room. My New Love asks, "Where are you going?"

I answered, "I'll be right back. I'm just going to the back room for a few minutes." I get to the room and closed the door quietly so that My New Love won't hear it close. I take the envelope out of my pocket and carefully open it. It was a letter from my Psvisor and it read like this:

'The little device you are holding in your hand is to call me anytime day or night. Just press the button on the side and I'll be there in no time no matter where you are. Just remember what I told you before that I have always wanted you the moment I set eyes on you. I know that you feel the same way but haven't fully realized it yet. But you will and soon.' I'm yours and yours alone.

I quickly put the little device back in my pocket and go back out to the living room. I sat down next to My New Love on the sofa. "It's so good to be home again," I said.

"I hate to ask," My New Love said, "But why did you go to the back room?"

I answered, "I just wanted to be alone for a moment and just feel the joy of being at home. I still can't believe that I'm out of the hospital and home for good."

My New Love pulls me close and wraps those arms around me. I glanced up at the clock on the wall and noticed how late it was getting. I got up and took a shower before going to bed. I didn't say a thing to My New Love as I went to bed and it didn't take long for me to fall fast asleep. It was a short time later when My New Love joined me.

It's about seven in the morning when I awoke to the bright sunlight and noticed that My New Love had already gotten up. I went to the kitchen to get something to drink and saw that there was a note on the counter.

It said the following: 'Had to be at work early and didn't want to wake you. Don't wait up 'cause I won't be home until sometime after dark, Your New Love.'

The note sounded cold which got me thinking about the note I got yesterday from Psvisor which was very warm. Should I or shouldn't I press that button on that little device? I eat something as I contemplated on what to do. I sat down at the chair next to the window and picked up the Party magazine. There was an article that caught my interest and I began reading it. It seemed that my mind kept wandering and couldn't concentrate on what I was reading even though I tried my hardest to do so. I got up from the chair and lay down on the sofa trying to clear those thoughts from my head. But it was no use, the harder I tried, the stronger they became.

I finally got up and pressed that button on the device. Within a few minutes, there was a knock on the door. I opened it and there in the doorway stood Psvisor.

"You and I both knew that you would press that button. I also knew that deep down you knew that you wanted me just like I wanted you and that you couldn't fight the overwhelming desire. As for My New Love, I arranged it so that the work shift would be very long today."

I just stood there speechless for a moment before I said, "Won't you come in." I closed the door behind us and went to the sofa with Psvisor. I started talking about how my day was going when I was suddenly cut short.

"I know you didn't just call me here to talk."

I understood what it all meant and was more than ready and willing for what was to come next. I placed my hand on the Psvisor's hand, squeezing it a little as I got up.

The Psvisor followed me down the hall to one of the bedrooms. I turned around and saw the pleased look on the Psvisor's face just as our lips touched and I felt the intense flame inside burn hotter than ever before. This is something I have never felt nor experienced with My New Love. We become *more* than one. No one else has taken me to this level before. It's a glorious feeling and what has been missing all this time from my life. This went on for hours and hours until we finally stopped and just laid there in each other's arms.

Psvisor whispers, "I'm going to take you even higher this time."

I didn't say a word, just smiled. That was all that was needed and this time we went higher. It was a mind-blowing experience that very few have ever felt. We kept this pace up all through the day and most of the night. I'm glad to never stop this wondrous feeling. Finally, we fell asleep sometime in the early morning.

I felt something brushing my neck which woke me up. It was the Psvisor who then suddenly pulled me on top and whispered, "You know what you want and what to do." I understood completely what Psvisor wanted and complied without hesitation. All my wants and

desires are fulfilled ten times over and I knew this will
be going on all day and night. Very few have ever had
this type of experience.

Chapter 17

I have been noticing lately that there has been a change in My New Love. I can't seem to figure out what has been happening. The feelings aren't as intense as they once were. I haven't said anything to My New Love yet but I need to soon because it is tearing me apart inside and I need to find out exactly what's going on which would put my mind at ease. This isn't going to be easy by no means and must be handled ever so delicately. I don't want to upset My New Love whatsoever. The rage would be intense and I would fear for my life.

It is early evening when we get home from work. It was a very uneventful day. There wasn't a whole lot for me to do but a couple of corrections on a book title. We sat down and had a nice, lite dinner. As we were sitting there, I was looking at My New Love and said, "We need to talk."

My New Love asked, "Is there something wrong?"

"I would rather discuss this after we have finished eating," I replied.

My New Love had a puzzled look but knew it had to be something really important for me to even wait until after dinner. We finished eating and went into the living room and sat down on the sofa. I looked in to My New Love's eyes and began speaking.

"I have noticed lately that you have changed and it isn't for the better. You seem more distant and I feel as if you no longer want me the way you used to."

My New Love took a moment before answering and said, "I'm sorry and didn't realize that has happened. I will always want you even when I take my last breath. I do have something to tell you and have been waiting for the right time. I know I can't keep this a secret any longer."

"You know that you don't have to keep any secrets from me."

"I know but I needed to find the right time and besides I couldn't tell you while you were recovering from the illness. I had to wait until you were well again."

My New Love could tell that I was starting to get a little agitated and just wanted to hear what needed to be said instead of avoiding the subject.

My New Love stuttered and stammered a little bit trying to find the right words and begins, "Remember on the last day before you were discharged that you had a final examination so you could be released from the hospital?"

"Yes. Why?" I replied.

"Well…I also went and had an examination. And well, ummm, errrr."

"Go on."

My New Love continues, "I am, uhh, how you say, pregnant."

"YOU'RE WHAT!" I exclaimed.

I just couldn't believe what I was hearing. This had to be some kind of joke. It's just not possible for such a thing to happen.

"Pregnant. But there's more. It's not yours, it's your Ex's child."

"It's what? Are you serious? I mean really. HOW COULD YOU DO THIS TO ME?"

My New love says, "I didn't mean for it to happen but it did and I'm so sorry. I didn't mean to hurt you in any way. It happened while you were in a comatose state."

I just sat there in total disbelief that someone would betray me in such a manner. I now realize that the dream that I had of the two of them together was real. At this point, I don't know what to think or feel. What is real and what isn't. I get up abruptly, not saying a word and went to the bedroom before My New Love had a chance to say anything else. I'm angry as hell but mostly upset that my Ex finally found a way to hurt me. Hurt me bad. I don't know if I'll ever get over this. I have no choice but to live with it since we are one and there's nothing I can do about it. The damage is done and I don't know if it can ever be repaired. I'm not sure exactly what to do next, how to feel much less carry on.

It was a little while later, My New Love comes into the bedroom where I am and tries to touch me. I turned away not wanting to be held, touched or anything. My New Love got the message and went back to the living room to sleep on the sofa leaving me alone again. This was fine with me. I finally fall asleep but tossed and turned not being able to find a comfortable position. Perhaps, I might subconsciously need to have My New Love next to me so I can get a restful sleep.

It's around two thirty in the morning when I wake up not that I was really getting any sleep in the first place. I decided to get up and go to the living room to check on My New Love. I could see that My New Love was asleep on the sofa and kneeled slowly onto the floor. I whispered softly and saw My New Love stir slightly and rolled over looking directly at me.

My New Love asked in a sleepy groggy voice, "What do you want?"

I answered, "I just wanted to apologize for how I acted earlier. It was so uncalled for but you need to understand why I had such a strong reaction."

"Go on. I'm listening."

I continued, "It was a real shock especially after everything I/we have been through. I know I overreacted. I hope you can forgive me."

"I do forgive you and my feelings for you have never changed. I figured that you needed some time to let this entire news sink in. I was just in as much shock as you were when I found out it wasn't yours," My New Love said.

Suddenly, I pulled My New Love towards me until our lips meet. You can feel the burning desire in both of us. My New Love pulled back a little bit and had a surprised look. It was the first time that I have ever done anything like this - taking the initiative.

My New Love exclaimed, "WOW! That was so unexpected and it has turned me on like never before."

Without saying another word, My New Love pulls me on top. With each thrusting movement, the burning desire is unlike anything we have experienced before. The ecstasy was so intense and the agony as sweet as the finest wine. Our bodies meld into one like never before. This went on for hours and hour's non-stop, so fantastic and mind-blowing, with no words to really describe it.

We finally fall asleep with me still on top and My New Love's arms wrapped tightly around me. I drift off into the most blissful sleep that I ever have had in my life.

It's about eleven o'clock the next morning when I finally stir. I look into My New Love's eyes and see that sly smile. I ask, "How long have you been awake?"

"Not for very long. I let you sleep in a bit longer and just didn't want this feeling to end," replied My New Love.

Suddenly, I felt a little strange and didn't know why. Before I could say anything else, My New Love spoke softly. "I have a surprise for you."

"What is it?" I ask.

My New Love answers, "The being I was carrying is inside of you now and is ours. What we did earlier erased any of your Ex's existence."

I kissed My New Love with so much fire and passion as we both tumbled to the floor from the sofa. We are still in each other as we begin again. All our senses are heightening to a new level that has been reached by only a few. One last thrust from My New Love and I let out a scream like I never have before. We fall back asleep for a little while. When I awake this time, My New Love was gently stroking my hair.

"There is one other thing I forgot to tell you," My New Love says in a soft gentle voice. "In a few weeks, I'll have to take you to the hospital where they will remove the being from you and take it to the nursery where it will be raised by Party Members whose only job is to raise children. We will not see this child ever again."

I understood completely, because this was how we all were raised. This way it is easier to have the offspring conform to the Party Doctrine. I will enjoy feeling what's inside me for the short time it will be there but I know that I will probably feel it forever and it is such a glorious feeling.

Chapter 18

It's time once again for the yearly Party Rally. I have been reading that this is going to be unlike any of the previous ones. I can't wait till Saturday when the big rally happens. All party members are required by the Doctrine that all free time will be used to help with set-up of the rally. No one seemed to mind helping. I oversaw setting up the chairs for the big rally. It took me several hours but I wanted to make sure everything was perfect.

Saturday is finally here and I got up really early. I was eager to get to the rally. I didn't care that it wasn't going to start for another couple of hours. The excitement and pride I felt for the Party was overwhelming. I found my seat in the front row. Just as I was about to sit down, someone from the Party Council came over to me and told me to follow which I did without questioning as to where or why. I had no idea why I was being summoned and of course it made me a little nervous. We arrived at an area where the other council members were seated and I was told to sit with them.

The head council member stood up and began speaking to me. "We have summoned you here because we have a very special citation that we will present to you during the rally. I cannot go into any further details at this time. Someone will come and get you at the appropriate time. For now, you are to just sit here and relax."

The council member sat back down and the rest cheered. I still had no idea what was going on. I could hear the speeches that were being made and enjoyed the intensity of what was being said.

One of the councilmen finally came and got me. Told me it was time. Time for what, I wondered. My question was quickly answered as I was escorted to the stage. I climbed up the stairs and told where to stand.

There was hush over the crowd as the Party Leader spoke and then introduced the head councilman who began speaking. "Comrades and council members, I want to introduce someone that exemplifies what it is to be a member of the party and the duty that is expected of them. This person has gone above and beyond what was expected without hesitation." The councilman turns to me motioning for me to come forward and stand up front. Then continues with the speech. "I give you the highest medal ever to be given to a non-official in recognition of the honor and duty you have demonstrated."

I stood there speechless as the crowd cheers feverishly and it felt so surreal. I looked out in the crowd to see if My New Love was there but to no avail. That disappointed and made me angry at the same time. How dare My New Love not be there to see me receive this honor? I was escorted off the stage and back to the room where I had waited. I sat there alone again when someone walked by. It was getting dark when I finally went home and was tired. I changed and went to bed. I didn't even notice if My New Love was home or not. At this point I really didn't care if My New Love ever did come home. As far as I'm concerned, we're through. I fell into a deep sleep and started dreaming, wondering if today's events really happened. I guess I'll know that in the morning.

It's about eight thirty when I awake on Sunday morning. I sat up on the edge of the bed and looked around. Something just doesn't look right. It doesn't look like my bedroom where I went to sleep last night. Maybe it's just my imagination playing tricks on me. I noticed that My New Love never came home last night. I let out a little sigh as I get up to go into the kitchen. I'm awfully thirsty this morning for some odd reason. I stopped suddenly at the end of the hallway. This *isn't* my apartment! Could I have accidently gone into the wrong one when I came home last night? That's just not possible. I have never made this type of mistake. I finally get to kitchen and make me some coffee. This should wake me up from this dream/nightmare.

As I finished drinking my coffee, I heard a knock on the door. I opened it and there stood two guards and another one I don't know. When one of the guards asked, "Do you know this person? They claim that they live here."

"No. I have never seen this person before," I replied.

The guard said, "That's what I thought."

They turned around and as I closed the door, I could hear the one I don't know yelling, 'BUT I DO LIVE HERE! You just got to believe me.'

That was strange I thought to myself. I went and sat on the sofa to reflect on what just happened and fell back asleep.

It must have been a few hours when I awoke. I looked around and didn't recognize anything. "WHERE IN THE HELL AM I?" I scream.

One of the guards came by and told me to be quiet, that if I yelled again I would receive a beating. I immediately did as I was told. There was this odor in the air that I recognized but have no idea from where or when or how I knew it. I looked around again and finally realized that I was in a cell. What have I done to be in this situation? How did I get here?

I could hear the guards marching in unison and what sounded like thunder when their boots hit the ground. I heard two guards coming toward my cell and one of them unlocked it. They motioned me to follow them. We walked down a long, dark hall before turning a corner and continued down a well lit one. We went into this room where I was told to lie down on a cold, metal table.

A nurse came in briefly and strapped me down. I was told that the doctor will be in shortly. Doctor? What? All these thoughts started racing through my mind. The doctor finally came in. Maybe now I could get some answers. Instead the nurse was instructed to put a needle in my arm which hurt like hell, then attached a bag of this greenish liquid which slowly dripped into my veins. It was the same type of liquid that I had seen in my nightmares.

It didn't take long for me to drift into a light sleep like state, as I did, I heard the doctor talking to the nurse saying this should help this patient with the madness. Madness? I know I'm not crazy. Or that's what I believe anyway. But it doesn't really matter what I believe, it's whatever they tell me as truth that I am supposed to accept, even though I know deep down they're lying.

Chapter 19

I have no idea how long I have been asleep but when I wake up, it isn't as it was before. The bed was soft not hard like the one in the cell. Someone is playing a cruel joke and I don't find it funny at all and who would do such a thing. I tried to get up but I couldn't seem to move and I have no idea why. I tried to call for someone to help me but no sound came out of my mouth. This is all so strange. I don't know what has happened to me and it is starting to scare me a bit – no, a lot! I knew I needed to get a grip and take charge of the situation - but how? - I can't move or speak. I could yesterday or so I thought. Maybe I'm just imagining all this – maybe this is another nightmare. I go back to sleep hoping this would all go away.

Suddenly, without warning I wake up and am running for my life through a hallway and out a door. I glanced back quickly and could see guards and dogs after me. What the hell is going on? This is becoming more and more bizarre. I dart into an empty building and hide. I could hear them go past and I just stayed where I was so they wouldn't find me. I heard someone shout, "OVER HERE!"

Before I could run, they grabbed me and dragged me back to that awful place. Before I knew it, I was in shackles and knew that this was the end. One of the guards removed the shackles if I promised that I wouldn't run or I would be shot if I did. I agreed and for my punishment, I was thrown into a dark, dank hole that had a foul stench. Is it that same hole I was in when these horrid nightmares began? I didn't care at this point, at least, I was alone. I must have fallen asleep and was awakened by one of the guards and taken to a cell to await my fate which will be decided in Magistrate Court. This is not looking good at all.

It was finally my time to appear before the judge. I was scared as hell as I was being escorted down what seemed like an endless hallway. We finally got to the court room and the judge looked so familiar. I know that face but maybe my mind is still playing tricks on me. I just sat there as all the charges were being read of what I had supposedly done. All I wanted to do was stand-up and scream that those were all lies. I didn't do any of those things; I dare not to say a word which could have made the whole situation worse than it already was. The judge finally called for a short recess and then came back within a few minutes. This is not looking good for me at all.

After both sides presented their case, the judge contemplated on what decision was to be made about my fate. The judge finally spoke, "Guilty of all 4th degree offences with extenuating circumstances and is eligible for special sentencing."

I was then motioned by one of the guards to follow the judge back to chambers. There was only the two of us as everyone else was dismissed. I kept wondering what my final fate was when I was told to sit in one of the chairs which I did immediately.

The judge began to speak as I listened attentively, hanging onto every word. "We have known each other on an extremely personal level. I also know that you didn't do any of those things but I had to find you guilty to appease the masses." The judge paused for a moment and then continued, "Your sentence is as follows: You are to be in my inner chambers from now on, undressed and ready for me."

The judge motioned for me to get up and follow. We went down this long hallway until we reached a door. The judge opened it and we went in. It looked like an apartment of some sort. "This is the inner chambers where you will stay. No one else knows about this place nor has anyone else ever been in here except for you today," the judge said.

It was quite clear on what it all meant. I quickly decided I could accept this; after all, it was better than a life in prison or worse, death! Without saying or thinking, I got undressed and proceeded to undress the judge who I could tell was enjoying it. I made sure my hands touched certain areas which drove the judge insane. The judge then took my hand as we knelt onto the floor with lips touching. I wasn't sure if I liked some of what the judge was doing or not. But I dare not say a word. Why ruin a good thing?

This went on for several hours until the judge got up to dress and says, "I'll be back in about an hour. I must hear a case and decide some poor fool's fate. I expect you to be as you are when I get back."

The judge leaves and I'm left alone to contemplate my next actions. I saw the ring on the judge's finger and realized it was My New Love. That is why everything felt so familiar to me. It is starting to make some sense I guess or at least it is in my mind.

I must have fallen asleep because now I am in my old apartment in my own bed. What is going on? This is incomprehensible! I was in the judge's apartment a few hours ago and now I'm not. I am so confused and disoriented; I have got to get my head cleared and figure out where I am, *when* I am! I glanced at the clock and noticed that I have very little time to get dressed to for work, if, in fact, I am back at the time when these nightmares began, I still work at the Litter-Dept. I think I do anyway.

As I walk to work, all I could do was keep thinking about all that has happened to me. As I am walking, things seem to look different or maybe it is just my imagination playing tricks on me. I have always gone this way to work. Did this really take place or was it some sort of bizarre dream that I had? I guess I'll never really know the answer. It seems that I have no concept of time anymore. I'm so unsure of anything. I finally get to work and sit down at my desk. I started sorting through a pile of papers getting them into some type of order. Someone comes by my desk and puts another stack of papers down. I noticed that there was an envelope on top. I wonder who it's from. I opened it and read, 'I hope you have…….' I dropped it immediately, looking all around and saw nothing unusual. Is this a joke someone is playing on me? Or am I starting this nightmare all over again?

Or – and this is the most frightening – HAVE THEY TAKEN ME! – AM I THEIR TOY??

Am I talking to you? Am I just crazy? Won't someone PLEASE help me!?